Harry's Hamster Hunt

T0318097

Written by Jane Clarke

Illustrated by Fran and David Brylewski

Collins

Who and what is in this story?

Listen and say

bookcase

Harry's dad

teddy

toybox

Harry's hamster

Download the audio at www.collins.co.uk/839698

Harry

Harry has a pet hamster.
It lives in Harry's bedroom.

The door is open. Harry can't see
his hamster!

Harry's hamster isn't there!

Harry needs to find his hamster.
Where can it be?

Harry looks for his hamster.
He looks under the bed.

Harry looks in the clothes basket.

Harry looks in his toybox.

Harry finds a lot of toys, but he can't find his hamster.

Harry has a bookcase. Harry likes books.
Harry's hamster likes books, too.

Harry looks on top of the bookcase.

Harry finds a lot of books.

Harry doesn't find his hamster.
The hamster isn't in his bedroom.

Harry looks for his hamster in the
living room.

Harry looks for his hamster on the sofa.

Harry finds an old sandwich.
He doesn't find his hamster.

Harry's hamster isn't in the living room.

Harry looks in the kitchen. He finds a lot of plates and bowls.

My hamster isn't here.

Harry finds a lot of cheese, but he doesn't find his hamster.

Cheese is Harry's favourite food.
Harry's hamster likes cheese, too.

Harry finds his hamster's favourite food.
Harry has a great idea!

My hamster loves this!

Harry can use the hamster food to find his hamster.

Harry is in the hall. He makes a long line of hamster food.

Come and get it, hamster!

Harry!

Harry's Dad is not happy.

Harry's dad wants to clean the floor.

Dad says, "Let's clean up all this hamster food!"

Harry doesn't think this is a good idea.

Harry and his Dad look in the machine.
They don't find the hamster. *Phew!*

Now, Harry is in bed.

He looked in the bedroom. He looked in
the living room. He looked in the kitchen
and he looked in the hall.

But Harry's hamster is lost.

Harry has a bad dream. A great big hamster finds him, and it sits on him!

Dad comes into Harry's bedroom.

Is everything ok, Harry?

Harry's hamster isn't lost now.

Harry didn't find his hamster.
His hamster found him!

Harry is very happy and so is his dad.
And so is his hamster!

Picture dictionary

Listen and repeat

bedroom

hall

hamster

kitchen

lost

under

1 Look and order the story

2 Listen and say

Collins

Published by Collins
An imprint of HarperCollins*Publishers*
Westerhill Road
Bishopbriggs
Glasgow
G64 2QT

HarperCollins*Publishers*
1st Floor, Watermarque Building
Ringsend Road
Dublin 4
Ireland

William Collins' dream of knowledge for all began with the publication of his first book in 1819.

A self-educated mill worker, he not only enriched millions of lives, but also founded a flourishing publishing house. Today, staying true to this spirit, Collins books are packed with inspiration, innovation and practical expertise. They place you at the centre of a world of possibility and give you exactly what you need to explore it.

© HarperCollins*Publishers* Limited 2020

10 9 8 7 6 5 4 3 2

ISBN 978-0-00-839698-5

Collins® and COBUILD® are registered trademarks of HarperCollins*Publishers* Limited

www.collins.co.uk/elt

British Library Cataloguing in Publication Data

A catalogue record for this publication is available from the British Library.

Author: Jane Clarke
Illustrator: Fran and David Brylewski (Beehive)
Series editor: Rebecca Adlard
Commissioning editor: Fiona Undrill
Publishing manager: Lisa Todd
Product managers: Jennifer Hall and Caroline Green
In-house editor: Alma Puts Keren
Project manager: Emily Hooton
Editor: Barbara MacKay
Proofreaders: Natalie Murray and Michael Lamb
Cover designer: Kevin Robbins
Typesetter: 2Hoots Publishing Services Ltd
Audio produced by id audio, London
Reading guide author: Emma Wilkinson
Production controller: Rachel Weaver
Printed and bound by: GPS Group, Slovenia

MIX
Paper from
responsible sources
FSC™ C007454

This book is produced from independently certified FSC™ paper to ensure responsible forest management.

For more information visit: **www.harpercollins.co.uk/green**

Download the audio for this book and a reading guide for parents and teachers at www.collins.co.uk/839698